Leprechaun Tales

Retold by **Yvonne Carroll**
Illustrated by **Jacqueline East**

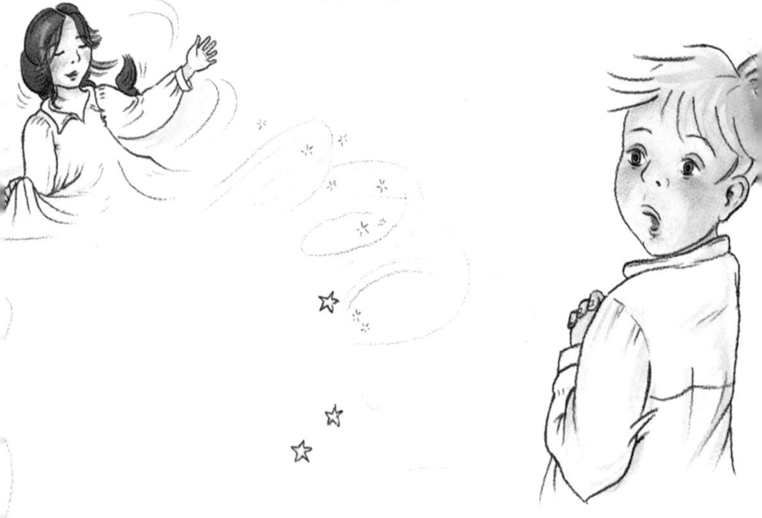

Gill Books

Contents

Gill Books
Hume Avenue, Park West, Dublin 12
www.gillbooks.ie
Gill Books is an imprint of M.H. Gill & Co.

ISBN 978 07171 2698 9
Printed in the EU

A CIP catalogue record for this book is available from the British Library.
5 4 3 2 1

Introduction

This selection of charming tales about Leprechauns and other "little people" has been passed down over the years from one generation to another. They have been a part of Irish folklore for hundreds of years.

Tradition has it that Leprechauns are mischievous little people, often cobblers, who have pots of gold hidden away. The humans are always keen to find the gold, of course, but somehow are always outwitted by the Leprechauns' cunning and magical powers. There is something for everyone to enjoy in these stories, especially the battle of wits between "them" and us!

The Crock of Gold

It was a clear moonlit night as Tom walked home from the village. Suddenly he heard a most peculiar sound coming from the bushes ahead. His mother had warned him to ignore strange sounds at night, as this was when the fairy people appeared. Even so, Tom paused for a moment before moving closer to the bushes to see what could possibly be making the noise.

He couldn't believe his eyes! There in front of him was a little man no bigger than Tom's hand, with his beard tangled in the bush. He wore brown trousers, a green waistcoat and a bright red cap on his head and his tiny shoes were on the ground beside him. He had something in his hand and when Tom looked at it closely he saw that it was an awl the size of a thimble.

"This is my lucky day!" Tom thought to himself. "I have found a leprechaun and every leprechaun has a pot of gold. I just have to keep him in sight and the gold will be mine."

Tom grabbed the leprechaun. He struggled, but Tom held him tightly and untangled his beard. This made the little man angry, but Tom ignored his bad temper and whistled a merry tune. All the while he made sure that he kept a firm hold on the leprechaun.

"Put me down," he shouted. "Not until you tell me where you have hidden your crock of gold," replied Tom. At last, when the leprechaun realised that Tom was determined not to let him go, he said, "Right, I give up. The gold is buried under this bush. Now let me go."

"Oh no!" said Tom. "I have no spade and if I go home now, how will I remember which bush is the one with the gold?"
"Why not mark the bush with your handkerchief?" suggested the leprechaun. "Of course!" agreed Tom, "but you must promise me that you won't take the gold when I'm gone."
The leprechaun promised, so Tom put him down and set off home.

The dawn was breaking by the time Tom returned. As he approached the bushes, what a sight met his eyes! Every bush had a bright red handkerchief tied to its lowest branch. "What a fool I was to let the leprechaun out of my sight," he whispered sadly to himself. "The gold will never be mine now."

Perhaps he imagined it, but as he slowly made his way home Tom thought he could hear the sound of laughter blowing on the wind.

Niamh

Niamh sat up in bed and listened carefully. There it was again! She had heard the sounds before, but this time she decided to investigate. She slipped on her dressing gown and made her way to the bedroom door. Down the stairs she crept. It was difficult to see because the only light to guide her was the light of the full moon that shone through the window. Just as she reached the kitchen door she knew that she was not alone.

It was her brother Liam. "Where are you going?" he whispered. "I heard the music again. This time I'm going to find out who is playing it. You can come with me," she replied. "But only if you do what I tell you." Liam didn't like to be told what to do, but he was a curious little boy and the chance of an adventure was too tempting to miss.

The children stood outside in the silver moonlight and listened. The music seemed no more than a whisper or a rustling of leaves. Was it the fairy people their grandmother had told them about? "Let's follow the path to the clearing in the wood," whispered Niamh. "I think that's where they meet." Liam agreed and they set off into the chilly night, full of excitement - and a little frightened as well.

A faint light flickered in the bushes as they approached the clearing. They could hear music - sweet, light music. Niamh couldn't decide what instruments were playing. She thought she could hear harps and flutes. It seemed as if the music was calling her. "Don't go too close," her brother warned. "Gran said that if the fairy people catch you, they'll keep you. Quick, let's go home."

Niamh crept closer and closer to the light. "Look!" she whispered excitedly. "Look! I was right all along!" Liam peeped through the branches. What a sight it was! Lights twinkled from the trees in the clearing. The children could see little people dancing in the centre. Gran's description of the leprechauns was perfect, right down to the silver buckles on their tiny shoes.

A new dance began with a faster rhythm. The music seemed to call them to join the dance. Liam remembered his Gran's warning to cover his ears. Niamh was spellbound. She began to move in time with the music. Suddenly there was a flash of light and Liam was blinded for a moment. When he opened his eyes again he was alone and his sister had vanished.

The search for Niamh went on for
a long time but there was not a
trace of her to be found.

Early one morning, many years later, Liam returned to the clearing in the wood. Although he now lived far away, he visited the spot where his sister had disappeared whenever he could.

As he approached he heard a child calling, "Liam! Liam! Where are you? We must go home." The voice was familiar. A little girl ran up to him and asked, "Have you seen my brother? We were dancing with the fairies and the leprechauns for twenty minutes and he's wandered off! It's time we went home."

Liam stared at her in amazement. "Niamh," he said, "Is it really you? You haven't spent twenty minutes dancing, you've been away for twenty years!"

The Sidhe

Once upon a time, a man called Sean lived in a small cottage near a small village. During the long winter nights the people of the village used to meet and tell stories or sing to pass the time. Sean loved the music and the stories, but unlike his family and neighbours he didn't believe in fairies or leprechauns or any of the little people. In fact, whenever he heard anyone talk about the Sidhe he would laugh and say that he couldn't understand how anyone could be so foolish as to believe that such stories could possibly be true.

One warm summer day, Sean was resting by the edge of his field. The air was filled with various sounds. He heard birds chirping and busy bees humming as they collected pollen. Suddenly, he became aware of another sound. It was a gentle tap-tapping which seemed to come from a nearby hedge. Sean moved forward slowly to investigate.

He couldn't believe what he saw before him! It was a real live leprechaun, exactly like those that Sean said didn't exist. The little man was there in front of him, sitting on a mushroom working hard. At his feet lay many different shoes, some with buckles, some dainty fairy slippers and some boots.

In a flash, Sean reached out and grabbed the little man. "Where is your pot of gold?" he demanded. "Gold!" said the little man crossly. "Gold! Where would I get a pot of gold? I'm only a poor shoemaker. All I have are my tools and this piece of leather."

"You can't fool me," said Sean. "Give me your gold and I'll set you free." "All right!" the little man cried. "My gold is buried safely in the field by the river. Take me there and I'll show you."

From the stories he had heard, Sean knew exactly what he had to do to get the leprechaun to part with his gold. He must not take his eyes off the man for an instant.

The leprechaun led him to a bush near the water's edge, in the next field. "There you are," he cried. "Take my gold." Keeping his eyes on the leprechaun, Sean reached into the bush. Suddenly he gave a scream of pain, for instead of a pot of gold he had put his hand into a bee hive!

Of course he looked to see where the bees were. As soon as Sean had taken his eyes off him, the little man vanished, just as the stories said he would.

Sean never told anyone how the leprechaun had fooled him when it was his turn to tell a story during the long winter nights. But no-one ever again heard him say that he didn't believe in fairies or leprechauns.

The Fairy Lios

One afternoon in early summer, Eithne and her brother Connor were playing in the field behind their house. Eithne was busy making daisy chains and then she decided to pick some of the wild flowers that were growing in the field. Her favourites were the bluebells. "Don't pick the flowers from the fairy lios, Eithne, or you will be sorry," her brother warned.

Eithne ignored his warning and continued to pick bluebells from the centre of the lios. "There are so many growing here that the fairies couldn't possibly notice if a few were picked," she answered.

The children returned home and Eithne put the bluebells in a vase on the kitchen table. As soon as their mother heard that she had picked them from the lios, she rushed outside and put them on the window ledge. She knew that if the fairy people were angry Eithne might be punished for interfering with the lios. And so she was!

When Eithne lay down in bed that night she jumped up screaming. Her bed was full of nettles! She tried to sleep in her parents' bed, but as soon as she lay down it too was full of stinging nettles. She tried Connor's bed but the same thing happened. "I'm sorry I ever went near the lios," she cried.

Her parents went to visit a wise old woman who lived nearby to ask what they should do. "The fairies will not be easy to please," she said. "But if someone in your family could do a good deed for them, perhaps they might remove the nettles."

The family thought and thought but what could they possibly do for the fairy people? At last, Connor had an idea. That night, he crept out of the house and went to the lios.

At midnight the lights twinkled in the lios and he could hear soft, light music. Connor loved music and he could play all sorts of tunes on his feadog (tin whistle). He recognised some of these tunes and thought to himself that it was strange that the little people should have the same music as mortals.

Cautiously, he pulled back the bushes and there in front of him were fairies and leprechauns dancing merrily! "The leprechaun has a whistle just like mine," he thought.

When the music stopped Connor moved forward. There was silence, then one of the leprechauns spoke angrily. "Your sister disturbed our lios and now you have come to disturb our dance." "No, no," said Connor. "I have come to tell you how sorry she is. I promise that she will never do such a thing again. Please take the nettles from her bed and let her sleep."

"Impossible!" said the leprechaun. "Go away before we punish you too." He turned to the musician. "Let the music start again!"

Connor stood outside the lios feeling very sad. It seemed that there was nothing to be done. His sister would never be able to sleep in a bed again. Then he had another idea.

Connor listened to the music once more. When the next dance was over and he thought that the piper was resting, he began to play a soft, sad tune. Playing his tune all the while, he parted the bushes and stepped into the lios. This time the fairy people listened.

He played for what seemed to be forever and when he finished, not a sound was to be heard. Then the applause began and the leprechaun who had spoken earlier spoke again. "Well played, Connor. You are a brave young man. We must reward you." "Oh no, I don't want anything for myself. I just want help for my sister Eithne."

The leprechaun turned to the others. They nodded. "Return home," he said. "We will grant your wish." Dawn broke and in an instant the lios was emptied as the Sidhe vanished.

When Connor returned home he found Eithne fast asleep in bed. His family knew that Connor had somehow broken the spell but they also knew that they could never ask how.

The Magic Cloak

It was almost dawn. Both sea and land were covered in mist. Eoin hid behind the rock as the tide ebbed far out into the bay. He had been waiting a long time for this special day. Every seven years a very strange magical event happened.

The old people in the village said that the sea went out as far as the horizon and the fairy people appeared. They spread a magic cloak in the centre of the sands and this held back the tide. Whoever owned the cloak could order the sea to stay back and would have good fertile land to make a farm.

Eoin always listened carefully to the stories the old people told, especially this one. Seven years earlier, he had crept out and watched in amazement as the waves rolled back and the fairy people appeared! This time he waited with his horse tethered nearby. At dawn they came. Eoin could hear the music of the fiddles and harps. Through the mist he could barely make out the shadows.

Slowly he got on his horse, making sure not to startle the animal. The mist lifted and once again Eoin saw the strangest sight before his eyes. The sea and sand had disappeared and in its place was a green plain as far as he could see.

Eoin knew what to do. He had to get the magic cloak - and the land would be his! But the cloak was guarded by leprechauns. He soon spotted them sitting in a circle, a pile of tiny shoes at their feet, tapping in time to the music. They were sitting on the cloak and the edges were flapping in the breeze.

Eoin pulled gently on the reins of his horse as they moved forwards. It took him longer than he expected to reach the cloak. When he looked back, it seemed that the shoreline was very far away in the distance.

As he came near to the leprechauns he slowed his horse and then dismounted a short distance away. He crept forward. He thought that they must hear his heart thumping or the sound of his breathing but no, they continued to work.

He reached out and, taking hold of a corner of the cloak, he pulled it from under them. Without delay he threw the cloak on his back, mounted his horse and galloped towards the shore. He could hear the chaos and confusion behind him but he dared not look back.

Suddenly all was quiet. It was an eerie quiet. The breeze dropped. "I've made it!" Eoin thought. Then he heard a rumbling noise. He looked over his shoulder and moving towards him with terrific speed was a gigantic wave. It was the Fairy Wave! Eoin urged his horse on but he was swept from the saddle. He felt as if he was being pulled in many directions and beaten by many pairs of hands.

As quickly as it had come the wave disappeared. When Eoin woke and tried to move, every bone and muscle in his body ached. "I've survived the Fairy Wave," he thought. "I have the magic cloak. I can control the sea. I'll be rich. I have beaten the fairies. I don't mind the pain." He put his hand on his back to feel the cloak but instead all he felt was a cloak of seaweed.

The New House

The children were very excited when they heard that they were going to move to a new house. Now that the twins were getting bigger, there didn't seem to be enough room in the cottage for all the family. The children were delighted to hear that their Granny would be coming to live in their old home. "That means that we will see her every day," said Ronan. The children loved their Granny and they especially loved to hear her stories. "We will have stories every day," said Sinead.

The family were very pleased
with the plans for the new house.
Everyone looked forward to the
day when the building would start
and each child planned how they
would decorate their own room.

One day Granny came to visit. The children told her of their plans and all was well until Granny asked where the new house was to be built. "At the top of the field near the cottage," replied Ronan. Granny didn't seem pleased to hear this. "It is a beautiful place to build a house, isn't it?" said Sinead. "We will be able to see the sea from the door and we will be able to visit you every day. Why aren't you happy, Granny?"

Granny hurried to speak to the children's father. "Eamon," she said, "you can't build your new house at the top of that field. The fairy people live there. No one must ever disturb those bushes in any way. Cut a single branch and you will never again have any luck!"

Eamon just laughed. "That's only an old story. No one believes stories like that any more!" He refused to listen to her.

The building began. Every day the children rushed home to see what had been built. Every night they talked and planned excitedly, but Granny never joined in the conversations.

There was great excitement the day the family moved into the new house. Eamon invited his friends and neighbours to a big party to celebrate. Most of the people he asked were delighted to accept, but some of the older people of the village thanked him and made excuses not to come. The party was held on a beautiful summer's evening. There was plenty to eat and to drink. Eamon had organized musicians and both young and old joined in the dancing.

At midnight, a breeze began to stir and soon it got stronger and colder until it became a howling wind. The sky grew darker. Suddenly, strange hammering noises came from inside the roof!

One by one the guests left. By now the noises were much louder and they seemed to come from everywhere – the roof, walls and chimney. The children were terrified. "It's the fairies and leprechauns!" they cried. Granny was right.

"We must go quickly, right now!" she cried. Eamon was the last to leave. He looked back and gasped! He could hear leprechauns hammering and smashing! The house shuddered and collapsed. Then the little people disappeared in a swirl of leaves.

Eamon and his family lived for many years in their little cottage. No one dared to touch the pile of bricks that had been their new house. After a time, the site was overgrown with hawthorn bushes and belonged once again to the fairy people.